Amish Romance Love Calls Me Close

Grace Given

Clean Christian Romance

PUREREAD.COM

Copyright © 2016 by **Grace Given**

All rights reserved. No part of this publication may be reproduced, distributed or transmitted in any form or by any means, without prior written permission.

Grace Given/PureRead Ltd
www.pureread.com

Publisher's Note: This is a work of fiction. Names, characters, places, and incidents are a product of the author's imagination. Locales and public names are sometimes used for atmospheric purposes. Any resemblance to actual people, living or dead, or to businesses, companies, events, institutions, or locales is completely coincidental.

This book is dedicated to YOU - the reader!
It is your encouragement and friendship, your emails, feedback and reviews, that make every one of these books so special!

NEVER MISS A NEW STORY
Want to be notified other Amish romance and mysteries by Grace Given? Sign up for New Releases and receive a free novella as a reward.

www.pureread.com/gracegiven

"But that on the good ground are they, which in an honest and good heart, having heard the word, keep it, and bring forth fruit with patience."
Luke 8:15

A PERSONAL WORD FROM GRACE

The Homeward Bound Amish Romance trilogy charts the challenging road that brings two hearts to their Sabbath rest of love for each other, and faith in Gott's will for their lives together.

"The world tells us that good things come to those who wait. But waiting is often the last thing we want to do, especially when the tender affections of our heart are involved. In this second book of the beautiful Homeward Bound trilogy, Sara has to choose her path - will she strive for the impossible love personified in the restless Zeke, or settle for the safety and security of faithful and gentle James.

In writing this story I was reminded of the Scripture in Romans 8:25, that speaks of hoping for that which we do not yet see, but that we do so with patience because something deep within us gives us assurance that somehow Gott will bring it to pass, if only we will believe and not doubt. I think this is the kind of faith that resides in our dear Sara's heart. It is the character of love tempered and tested by trial."

Grace Given, Author

Contents

The Perfect Work 1
Slow to Anger 9
Burning Hearts 15
Faithful 21
The Purposes of Gott and Man 29
Return 37
Speaking Truth 47
Peace and Good Will 53
The Mission of the Heart 61
Bonus Chapter – Homeward Bound Book 3 67

CHAPTER ONE

The Perfect Work

"BUT LET PATIENCE have her perfect work, that ye may be perfect and entire, wanting nothing."
James 1:3

Sara Miller trembled as she directed the horse away from the Breneman farm, and from Zeke Breneman. The crisp evening air added to her chill. Zeke was the last person she expected to see. The man she saw coming back to his home was barely recognizable. Bent shoulders and the despondency in his face covered the person she once knew so well. Thinking of her first response to his question concerning her presence at his home caused Sara to wonder about her answer.

Never before had she abandoned a neighbor in need. And yet, she told him his mother would need someone to help her when she returned home from the hospital the next day. At any other time, it was expected she would continue to take care of things for Ruby and Jonathan's family. Their son, Eli, had all he could do to keep things going outside with his father. Until this night, their only other child was gone from them. Sara shook her head and slowed the horse down to a reasonable pace.

"I cannot go back to that house," she said aloud. "Zeke disappeared without a word to me and now he simply walks back in as if we saw each other the day before."

Anger crept up within her. She must pray for calm and direction the rest of the way home. Anger was not the answer. Her brother Perry saw her coming up the road. He went outside and took care of the horse and buggy. Concern showed in his eyes when he looked at her.

"You must be cold, Shveshtah," he said. "Go inside and warm yourself. Maemm has a hot supper waiting."

Sara drew in the aroma of a delicious beef stew on the stove. The table was set and her mother had everything ready. Sara told her she should have waited for her to help her.

"You have your hands full, Sara," said Emma. "Everything is ready."

She took her daughter's hand and wrapped comforting warm ones around it. Mother and daughter smiled at each other. Peace and security flooded over Sara. Everything was going to be all right, she thought. Tonight I will focus on my loving family. Tomorrow I will deal with Zeke's reappearance.

"How is Ruby getting along?" asked her mother.

Sara told her their neighbor would be home the next day. She did not mention Zeke's return and was glad when the subject of the Brenemans moved on.

"Winter will be here before we know it," said her father. "I am glad we baled enough hay for the season. Our animals will be fine and healthy." He looked at his wife and daughter. "We will be taken care of as well, thanks to my wife and daughter. It looks as if we have plenty of vegetables and fruits stored in jars. The meat is in the smokehouse. We are ready."

Her father was right. Sara had much to be thankful for. She laughed aloud when she watched her youngest brother more interested in his food than concerns about their welfare. "Jacob, you will soon be eleven. That means you will have to do more to help out."

Jacob stared at his sister. "I already help out. I can milk the cows and I helped Perry with the haybaler." He looked at his father. "That is right, isn't it Daed? I do my part."

Eli kept a serious face. "You have learned much, Jacob. You will be a fine farmer some day."

Later that night as Sara prepared for bed, Zeke seized her thoughts. She wondered what had happened to him while out in the world. He had been gone for two months. He intended to travel the world and then become a writer. His desire to write about the outside world was something she did not understand. She tried to recall what he carried with him when he suddenly appeared in the near darkness that evening. Sara recalled his face and broken body. She had no memory whether he carried anything with him or not.

Her love for him remained but she could not afford to dwell on her heart and feelings. He betrayed her once and until she was convinced of his steadfastness she needed to keep her distance from him. She prayed for the ability to take one day at a time on the matter and for her Gott to take control of her feelings.

The next morning Sara helped her mother prepare breakfast. After her father and brothers came in from the barn they bowed their heads in prayer and then ate hearty breakfasts. The boys left for school and her father returned to his chores. Sara began clearing the table.

"I will take care of this, Sara," said her mother. "You should get on over to the Brenemans. You'll have to prepare for Ruby. She will need some furniture rearranged and things like that. I wonder if she will be in a wheelchair or use a walker."

Sara did not respond at first. "I am not going today," she managed to say at last.

"Is someone else taking over for a while?" asked Emma.

"I do not know but they will have to find someone else to help them."

Emma scrutinized her daughter. Sara's face was drawn. Perhaps the extra work of the past week was too much for her. It was the first time extra work took its toll on her daughter, thought Emma. No, that was not it. Something happened over there.

"What is it, Dochtah? Did something happen that makes you refuse to help our neighbors?"

Emma could not imagine why Sara did not want to go. She followed the Amish ways of helping those in need and now she refused to do that. Ruby Breneman would need a lot of help until she was on her feet again. When her daughter answered her, she was astounded at the news.

"Just as I left last night, Zeke walked up the lane. He is home again."

Sara rested her hands on the edge of the counter and looked down at the floor. Emma took in the words in a thoughtful manner. The Zeke who Sara fell in love with was back. Her mother hoped he would not tear her daughter's heart apart as he did before. There was no doubt Sara still loved him but now that he was here she did not want to face him. Both women were silent for a few minutes.

"He does not look the same," said Sara. "I have no idea what he went through but he looked like a shattered man. I still love him, Maemm, but I'm not sure I am in love with the real man or not." Her eyes pled with her mother. "I cannot face him yet."

Emma Miller knew her daughter had a long road ahead of her to figure things out. She would excuse her this one time from assisting a neighbor in need. She removed her apron and hung it on the hook by the door.

"I will go to the Breneman house today. You take care of things here. Pray hard, my Dochtah. You cannot run away from things. You will find the strength you need."

Emma pulled on her warm boots and wrapped her woolen coat around her. Eli had the buggy ready for her. He did not question his wife's decision. They would talk privately later.

Sara felt remorse that her mother stepped in for her. She was right about not running away from problems. She should have gone and faced Zeke. The sooner the better, she thought. But for today she was glad her mother gave her time to think things over.

It was only then that Sara thought of James Bernhard. After Zeke left for the outside world, James entered her life. He had waited patiently for his chance to court the woman he loved since their school days. He found it hard to focus on anything except her at the socials and in church. The day Sara lost Zeke was the day James' hopes soared. It had taken several weeks before he began courting her. He knew her heart still held love for Zeke. James was patient, and at first, he felt she would come to love him the way he did her. That day was yet to come.

Sara knew James well enough to know that once he learned Zeke was home again, he would not be happy. James was wonderful. He was kind, considerate and baptized into the church as she was. They had more in common than the wild ways of Zeke and his goals. She wanted to live the life of an Amish wife and mother. James wanted the same thing as a husband and father. Both were devoted to their community and church. It was rumored James was considered for a position in the church as Deacon. Sara and James were good friends. The one thing that separated them was the fact he loved her, but she did not love him.

More than once, Sara knew she must be honest with James. It was wrong to lead him on in the courtship. She deprived him of the chance to court someone else who would make a better wife for him. He deserved someone who could return his love the way it was meant to be.

Zeke was not baptized and so not a church member. She wondered if he would study for baptism now that he was home.

Hopes and desires rushed through her until she recalled his betrayal when he left without a final word to her. His expressions of love prior to that day meant nothing when she learned of his actions.

CHAPTER TWO

Slow to Anger

"WHEREFORE, MY BELOVED brethren, let every man be swift to hear, slow to speak, slow to wrath: For the wrath of man worketh not the righteousness of God.
James 1:19-20

The night before, Jonathan Breneman had placed the wrapped warm bricks under Sara Miller's feet in the buggy. She was a Godsend to his family. He marveled at her ability to cook and take care of the house as if her own. She was in her element when it came to that. Saddened by his son's desires to go out into the world, rather than marry Sara Miller, pierced him deeply. Zeke's duties were right here where he belonged. Now, more than ever they needed him. Ruby would be incapacitated in her duties for a while before her hip healed.

When he stepped back from Sara's buggy he noticed alarm on her face. He followed her gaze to the figure walking up the lane. The man's appearance was changed but there was no doubt his son was home. He wanted to run to meet Zeke and pull him to him, but he stood back and allowed Sara to speak the first words. Her words were as crisp as the night air in her greeting. He could not blame her. His son hurt her badly. As much as Jonathan hoped they would settle down and marry, he was happy when James Bernhard began courting her. She deserved a good man like him.

Jonathan recalled how adamant Zeke had been when they spoke their last words together. Until now he doubted they would ever see one another again. Ruby Breneman lived daily with the knowledge her prayers would be answered and her eldest son would return home to his family. Ruby's homecoming the next day held an unexpected surprise for her.

The next morning, Jonathan and his son Eli came into the house. Breakfast was not on the table as usual. Emma Miller turned and smiled at the two. She apologized for being late and finished the meal preparation without a word as to why she was here rather than her daughter. Jonathan did not object. He knew very well why Sara did not come.

"You probably already know this, Emma, but I want you to hear it in my words," said Jonathan.

"Zeke came home last night. He will be in soon. He is finishing at the barn."

Emma nodded and set the bacon, eggs and pancakes on the table. She reached for the coffee pot and poured coffee into three cups. While they ate she prepared for Ruby's homecoming. The footsteps heard behind her caused her to turn to Zeke Breneman. She managed to hold a gasp that wanted to escape her throat when she saw him. He was pale and thin. She wiped her hands on her apron and smiled at him.

"Willkomm home Zeke. I am very glad to see you. It will be a gut thing for your Maemm to have you here when she gets home today."

Only his lips held a smile in greeting. His eyes held defeat. Sympathy swirled through Emma. The man before her had much healing to do. She told the family she would prepare the sitting room for Ruby while they ate.

"Eli and I moved our bed downstairs for her last night," said Jonathan. "She will not be able to manage the stairs."

They discussed other things to provide comfort for Ruby. Emma put a plan in motion for the community to rotate days to help the family. All agreed to it. Even Zeke expressed gratitude for the help of neighbors. That was a good sign that he would learn to fit back into the Amish way of life, thought Emma. That is where his security and love is. Ruby was not the only one in the family who would benefit from the generosity of others. Everyone would rejoice that one of their own returned home to them.

Emma spent the rest of the morning getting the house in order. Another neighbor would arrive early afternoon to help her with the laundry. Between the two of them, things should go smoothly. Ruby was due home mid-afternoon. Jonathan hired a driver to take him to pick her up from the hospital.

Sara kept busy with laundry at home and other chores necessary to keep things running in good order. The bitter wind whipped her body as she hung clothes on the line. The sun was out and she was grateful the clothes would dry quicker. There won't be many days left like this one, she thought. No matter how many times she introduced new thoughts to her mind, Zeke loomed larger than any of them.

"I cannot avoid him forever," she said to the wind. "The day must come that we face one another."

Once the washing was finished, Sara began preparing supper. Jacob and Perry arrived home from school and immediately went to the barn to help their father. Dusk inched in taking the sunlight away in preparation for the night. The rhythmic clip-clop of the horse sounded pleasing to Sara. She glanced out the kitchen window as her mother stepped to the ground and pulled her woolen coat tighter. Perry approached to take care of the horse and buggy. Emma's sense of smell enhanced at the aroma of fried chicken in the iron skillet. White potatoes boiled in the large pot and fresh bread on the plate was covered with a white dish towel.

"You are a Godsend, Dochtah," she said. The rush of cold air lasted a few seconds before she closed the door behind her. "Everything smells gut."

Sara smiled at her mother and took her coat from her. "I have a cup of kaffe ready for you. Sit down and have some while you warm up." Emma's fingers curled around the warm cup. It is gut to be in my own home, she thought.

During the evening meal Emma told her family of Ruby Breneman's return home from the hospital. "She is doing very well," said Emma. "I do not believe anything will keep her down for long."

She looked at Sara and quickly returned her eyes to the food on her fork. Before she took a bite, she said, "Zeke is home and he gave the most happiness to Ruby."

Eli and her sons stopped eating. To fill the awkward moment, Sara decided to speak.

"I am glad he returned home. It is where he belongs."

Relieved that her daughter broke the tension, Emma told them of various neighbors who were lined up to take turns at the Breneman house. The plan meant neither Miller woman was due to go back for another five days.

When Sara's head rested on her pillow that night, she whispered a prayer for Zeke and his family. She thanked her Gott that the earlier anger dissipated. She vowed to speak with Zeke the next day. Calm washed over her before she drifted off to sleep.

CHAPTER THREE

Burning Hearts

"MY HEART WAS hot within me, while I was musing the fire burned: then spake I with my tongue"
Psalm 39:3

The loud knocking on the Miller's door brought everyone out of their rooms. Eli told his family to wait while he found out what was going on.

"Someone is in trouble," said Emma. "We will pray." Her three children bowed their heads while their father answered the pounding on the door.

Eli called for his family. "There has been more trouble for the Breneman family. Their barn caught on fire. Perry, come with me." He told them Eli Breneman brought the bad news. Perry hitched the horse to the open wagon and threw in numerous large buckets for water.

There were times barns were saved, but often they burned down in spite of water being thrown on the flaming structures. Sara thought of their barn that now housed the cows on one end and two horses at the other end. If not for the cold nights, all animals would be in the pasture. She did not doubt the Brenemans brought their animals in for the night as well. She and her mother began their work. Sara made a large pot of coffee while her mother gathered blankets for warmth. There was no time to warm bricks for the ride to their neighbor's farm.

"Jacob, you must help us, too," said Emma.

Her young son was upset his Daed did not ask him to come with him and his brother. He forced a smile. "You must hitch the horse to the second buggy. Go now."

Sara poured the coffee into a large crock and wrapped a thick towel around it. In short time, everything was ready. The hot coffee and the Millers were in the buggy. The air was colder than earlier. Numerous stars blanketed the sky.

When the Breneman farm came into view, they saw flames that no longer leaped into the night sky. They smoldered nearer to the heap of seared beams and ashes on the ground. Other buggies were at the scene. Women unloaded hot drinks for the firefighters. They quickly handed steaming liquids to the men who stood back and realized the barn was destroyed. Everyone spoke of plans to build another one for their neighbor.

Sara met Zeke's eyes. His face, like the other men, streaked with soot. He sat down on the top step of the porch. Sara poured hot coffee for all of them. She was grateful Esther Clodfelter filled Zeke's cup.

"We lost a cow and her calf," said Jonathan. He looked at everyone around him. "That is a small loss thanks to all of my gut neighbors."

When the Miller family returned home, it was time to take care of their own animals. The boys and their father hurried to the barn. Sara and Emma started scrambling eggs. Breakfast would be heartier than usual. Emma smiled when she noted how hungry the three were when they came from their chores. Once the meal was eaten, Jacob and Perry got ready for school and hurried toward the schoolhouse.

Without words, Emma and Sara were glad to have a day of normal tasks. They discussed plans of what to cook for the day of the barn raising.

"I miss seeing Esther," said Sara. "I know with her job as teacher she has little time left for visiting."

Sara knew that her best friend's day did not end when she finished teaching the children. She had a full day's work waiting for her at home. The petite woman's stature belied her strength and resolve. At age seventeen, Esther took over most of her mother's chores. Ruth Clodfelter's health declined slowly. Her brother Silas was married to a generous woman who gladly helped her husband's family. They lived several miles away and it was not easy to make the trip. Marian took care of her family's laundry on Monday and came to her in-laws house on Tuesdays to take care of their laundry. Marian and Silas were expecting their first child in early spring.

Esther's other brother, Isaac, age fifteen worked hard with her father, Jacob Clodfelter. In spite of Esther's workload she remained cheerful. In warmer weather she often stopped to visit Sara on her way home from the schoolhouse.

"The nights come early now, Sara. Esther does not have time," said her mother. "Perhaps you and she can visit this Sunday. We will not have services this week. It will be gut for both of you."

"I will tell James I plan to visit Esther this Sunday. Perhaps he will agree to take a buggy ride Saturday night instead."

Her mother laughed. "He may prefer a visit with you inside where it is warm." Her daughter agreed that may be best. Emma wondered how much longer her daughter would continue seeing James now that Zeke was back. Something was missing between the gut man and her dochtah. Emma was certain Sara's heart still set on Zeke

Breneman. She prayed Sara would make the right decision regarding the man she should marry.

Sara sent a message with Perry to give to his teacher. Sara's Sundays had been taken up with James Bernhard. James was someone else she must talk with. He obviously loved her deeply. She enjoyed his friendship and knew it was wrong to keep leading him on. Before Zeke returned she had almost agreed to marry James. There was nothing to dislike about James. But Sara knew love completed a happy marriage.

The only way to find out if possibilities for her and Zeke still existed was to face him. Now that the barn burned down, Zeke and Eli would be busy today building shelter for the remaining animals and cleaning up the aftermath of the fire. Neighbors would help with the cleanup as well. Sara wondered at the tribulations asked of the Breneman family. The loss of the animals was major enough but now their mother depended on others to do her normal chores. And there was Zeke for them to be concerned about. The family demonstrated deep faith and trust in their Gott; all except Zeke, thought Sara. She silently prayed verses from her Bible.

Visions of the hollow look in Zeke's eyes caused shivers to pulse through her.

CHAPTER FOUR

Faithful

"MOST MEN WILL proclaim every one his own goodness: but a faithful man who can find?"
Proverbs 20:6

Ruth Clodfelter's eyes fluttered and closed again. Jacob bent over his wife and encouraged her to wake up. She met his eyes and waited for him to speak. He told her of their neighbor's disaster.

"Esther told Jonathan Breneman she will take the geese and care for them until another barn can be raised. There are three horses that needed shelter as well."

Jacob hoped the subject would divert his wife's despondency. Instead, a slight fire lit her eyes.

"How does Esther have time to take care of geese," she said. "I hope you did not allow her to bring the horses here as well."

"She will not bring the horses here. The Kauffmans took them. There is no reason to not help our neighbors. They would all do the same for us, Ruth. We both know that very well."

When Esther brought her mother's breakfast to her room before leaving for school, Ruth turned her head away and refused the food. Esther smiled and told her to eat when she felt better. Ruth refused most meals and Jacob wondered if she wanted to die. He shook his head at thoughts like that. It was not the Amish way to purposefully take one's own life in any manner. His prayers at night became more fervent than ever for the healing of his wife. The Amish group who dealt with matters of the mind seemed to help her at first. Then she refused to go for the sessions after the first two. His Bishop advised him to leave it in the hands of Gott and to continue to pray for her.

Jacob took a deep breath and asked his wife if she needed anything. She turned her head away from him and closed her eyes. He left the room and returned to help Isaac chop wood. He was glad Esther and Letty were at the schoolhouse all day. He smiled when he thought of his daughters. Esther was a mother to his seven year old little one but he worried that she shunned men who wanted to court her. He felt in his heart that was because she felt obligated to take over duties his wife should be fulfilling.

Saturday night arrived and Sara told her mother she and James were going to take a short ride in the cold air. James noticed a more serious Sara than usual. If she planned to talk about the two of them, he was ready to do so. James took her hand and helped her into the boxed buggy. He settled the warmed bricks around her feet and handed her an extra woolen blanket. They rode off, silent at first. Then James spoke.

"Sara, I think we must talk about serious things tonight." She nodded in agreement. "I must ask you about your feelings for me. I know that with Zeke back home perhaps your heart is still with him?"

Mortified at his words, Sara appreciated the matter getting out into the open.

"I have not spoken with Zeke alone since his return. You deserve honesty from me, James," she said. "In my heart I still hold a place for him. I do not know if our feelings are mutual ones or not. I want to talk with him and find out directly from him."

"Do you hold any true feelings of love for me?" asked James.

The wind picked up but neither one of them noticed.

"I value you as a very gut friend, James. You are considerate and respectful toward me. You are someone who will make a very gut husband and father. I want to be that person for you, but at the same time I know you deserve more than friendship."

Sara reached for his arm and felt strong muscles. Her touch sent hope through James.

"I love you Sara. You are right when you say friendship alone is not strong enough for a marriage without love." He paused before saying words he did not want to say, but must be said anyway. "I think that I should not continue the courtship until you know your heart. You must settle things one way or another with Zeke."

Tears sprang to her eyes. Doubts swirled through her head. What if Zeke was not the man she thought he was and she lost the man next to her? She took a deep breath to steady her voice.

"You are right. It is the only fair way. I will not let this go any longer, James. In this next week I will know how Zeke and I stand. But I do not expect you to stand by and wait for me."

That night as she prepared for bed, Sara looked forward to talking with her best friend, Esther. They had much to catch up on and Esther would benefit from a break from her duties at home.

She awoke Sunday morning to light snow drifting down. By noon the snow stopped and bright sunlight filtered through the house. The family gathered in the sitting room and Jacob pulled a game off the shelf.

"Not Life on the Farm again," said Perry.

Everyone laughed. Emma suggested a game of Scrabble instead. She thought it would be a good one and Jacob was old enough to come up with enough words to build.

"We will play Scrabble," said Eli. "Then we'll get the buggy ready and visit the Kauffmans and others today. The snow has stopped and the sun is out." Jacob and Perry looked at him with expectancy. "All right," said their father. "We will go now and save Scrabble for another Sunday."

The boys rushed to the barn to hitch the horses. Eli and Emma laughed at them. They were grateful their children were all healthy.

"What about you, Sara?" asked her father.

"Esther will be here soon. We will spend the afternoon together."

As soon as her family left Sara saw her friend coming down the lane. As usual Esther jumped out of the buggy with enthusiasm and tied her horse to the hitching post. They hugged and walked into the house. Sara offered kaffe to her and they sat down in front of a plate of sweet rolls.

"Your Maemm bakes the best sweet rolls in the country," said Esther.

"Why danka, but I made those rolls this morning," said Sara.

The light banter between them soothed both women. Esther asked Sara if she had talked with Zeke since his return.

"I have not had more than a short greeting with him. No matter what happens I will talk with him in the next few days."

Sara told her friend about James' words the night before.

"He does deserve to know where you stand," said Esther. "Do you still love Zeke as much as you did before he left?"

Sara was silent. The question put that way, caused her to analyze the answer better. Esther reached for her hand and squeezed it.

"He appears very different," said Sara. "I believe something out in the world changed him."

"I agree he is not the same person. Perhaps he will tell you of his experience and you can go from there."

Sara jerked her head upright. "I must not speak of things of the world, Esther. You know that."

Esther wrapped both hands around Sara's. "Sara, you must speak of those things with Zeke. It will be between the two of you. How else will you know how he feels? You must find out everything you can if you want to make a true decision about your life."

After a few more words, Sara agreed with her friend.

"James Bernhard is very handsome," said Esther. The twinkle in her eyes lifted the mood of the room. "He will be a gut catch for someone if you do not take him."

An unexpected warmth and peace seared through Sara. "He is one of the best unmarried men in the community," she said. "Do you think love can grow from friendship?"

Esther laughed. "After all of this time with him, you should know that answer. Let's get out into the cold air and clear our heads." She pulled her friend to her feet. "Cold air has a way of ridding the mind of cobwebs."

"Before we leave, let us pray together."

The snow did not stick on the ground and the two women walked the pathway to the creek. They did not speak of concerns but marveled at the beauty of late fall. Winter would arrive in two weeks though nature pushed it early.

"My Daed allowed me to take the small flock of geese to our barn for the Brenemans," said Esther.

Sara knew Esther preferred animals to household duties. "I am surprised you have time to take care of geese."

"I am making time for them. They do not take much care. Jonathan sent grain home with me for them. The barn raising will be this coming Saturday."

They talked of the barn raising. The event was a social to look forward to. Everyone planned food to bring and the house would be cleared and tables set up. The women talked of Ruby's dependence for help.

"Eli told me she is ready to walk on her own again, but I am not so sure she can do much," said Esther. "Knowing her spirit, she will be right in there with the rest of us."

Sara agreed with the assessment. Depending on others was not something Ruby Breneman handled well though grateful for everyone's help.

CHAPTER FIVE

The Purposes of Gott and Man

*"WITHOUT COUNSEL PURPOSES are
disappointed
Proverbs 15:22*

Monday afternoon when laundry was finished, Emma told Sara to take a break before time to begin the evening dinner. She told her mother she had an errand to do and would be back soon to help her.

Sara was ready with the enclosed buggy and wrapped blankets around her legs and feet. She headed for the Breneman farm. When she pulled up to the hitching post, she saw Zeke near the burned barn. He and Eli were cleaning up debris. She would never interrupt a workday like this but the matter between her and Zeke could not be delayed any longer.

Eli saw her first and poked his brother who watched the woman alight from the buggy. They met in the side yard.

"I am interrupting your work, Zeke. I know there is much to do but we must talk now. There is no waiting."

Zeke brushed his gloved hands on the side of his pants and nodded. They walked together toward the unfenced pasture a half mile from the Breneman house. Sara wrapped her coat tighter.

"Why did you come back?" she asked.

"I was wrong about my place in the world outside," he said. He knew he owed her more than she asked. "At first I found a job in an art studio. The owner was very nice to me and taught me how to arrange works in the store. I learned how to label the prices and how to greet customers. I planned to work there until I had enough money to travel farther west. Someone came in one day and recognized me from my rumspringa days."

Sara did not say anything. She expected him to continue until she knew everything.

"I know you are against talking about things like this," said Zeke.

"I want you to tell me everything. I will listen."

"The man's name was Jason McCauley, an Englischer. I recalled he was in the library a few times when I was there. He liked literature and took college classes. He came in to use reference books for one of his classes. The day he came into the art studio, I learned he had graduated with a degree in Journalism."

Sara barely felt the wind whipping her face. "What happened then?" she asked.

"By that time, I had a little money saved up. Looking back, I should have waited until I had more. Jason wanted to take me to dinner that night. He said he had something to discuss with me. We went to a small restaurant and I listened to what he had to tell me."

Zeke did not mention the restaurant was a bar and grill. He and Jason drank a beer or two and ate overloaded sub sandwiches and pretzels while they talked. By the end of the evening, Zeke agreed to go with Jason to the Wyoming. He convinced Zeke he had enough money to go and when they arrived in Jackson Hole there was a job at a newspaper office waiting for Jason.

"He told me not to worry about money. He had enough to get us out there and that there were plenty of jobs there for me while I worked on my writing. I flew on a plane for the first time to Jackson Hole the next week. Jason paid for everything, including the airline ticket."

"It all sounds as if that was what you wanted," said Sara.

"I thought so, too," said Zeke. His voice did not hold enthusiasm but rather bordered on sarcasm. Sara looked quickly at him. "I mean I had high hopes. There were the majestic mountains I only read about. The wild animals were amazing to me. I roomed with Jason in a two-bedroom apartment and found a job at a Souvenir shop."

Again, Zeke did not give details. The shop sold cheap articles that were factory made. The Englischers bought trinkets to take back home with them. Zeke often wondered what they did with them once home. His boss told him not to worry about things like that. His interest was in how much they bought. He often told Zeke it was the bottom line that was important. Everything in Jackson Hole seemed to be about money in the midst of all the natural beauty. Deep inside Zeke felt there was something very wrong with attitudes like that.

"Sara, I was not happy there. When I came back to the apartment in the evenings I found I could not write anything at all. No one saw the surrounding beauty as I did. Jason found a girlfriend and he was home less and less. He continued to pay his share of the bills but I knew I needed to do something else."

Sara noted a deeper pink slowly cover Zeke's face. The tint was deeper than results of the cold air. She encouraged him to continue.

"My boss at the shop did not respect his customers. He had a young son age eight. Steven came to the shop after school each day. The man spoke very bad words in every sentence, even in front of his young son. He was not someone I wanted to work for. At the time, I had no other prospects for a job."

Zeke told her of the increasing tourists who arrived for skiing. He described the heavy snows and the ski trails in the mountains. Sara did not miss his enthusiasm when he spoke of the beauty of Wyoming. At the same time, she knew he had no respect for the Englischers in the region. He spoke of their expensive clothing, their endless flow of money and most of all, their demands for better service no matter what store or restaurant they patronized.

"I wanted the environment nature offered but the outside world is filled with selfish people. If I stayed, perhaps I would have finally joined up with some true friends. Something else happened that clinched it for me that I should not be out there."

They turned to go back toward the farmhouse. The wind whipped furiously and snow began to fall. Sara looked up at the sky and then her eyes grazed over all that nature offered right here.

"We live in a beautiful place," she said. "Just watch the snow fall. Do you remember when we were taught that every snowflake is different and no two are alike? That is the work of Gott in nature."

Zeke laughed for the first time. "Yes, I do recall that. Later I thought that fact was from science, something not allowed in an Amish schoolhouse."

"I think it was learning of the creativity of our Gott, not science," said Sara.

Zeke had no words in answer. His mind was not yet settled back into the ways of the Amish. Again, he wondered if he and Sara would ever connect in mutual thoughts and goals. Writing about the beauty of the world was something he doubted would ever be far from his aspirations.

His dilemma was he wanted the best part of two worlds: opportunity to fulfill his dreams as a literary writer and the security of his Amish family and community. Most of all, he wanted to share his life with Sara Miller.

As they got closer to where Eli and his father worked on the clean up, Sara said, "We have much to talk about still, but I cannot keep you from your work, Zeke." He agreed they would talk again soon.

Sara left him to his tasks. On her way home, her heart felt empty. Nothing had been resolved between them. She tried not to think of Zeke's words. The tone of his voice when he spoke of the beauty in Wyoming told her his ambitions were the same as before he left.

It was much later that Sara realized Zeke had not explained what happened to cause him to come back home.

CHAPTER SIX

Return

"HE OPENETH ALSO their ear to discipline, and commandeth that they return from iniquity."
Job 36:10

Zeke joined his brother in the work of cleaning up the barn area. He wanted to finish his story of the outside world with Sara but when she spoke of the snowflakes he did not want to mar her face with sadness. Unfinished business remained between them. His younger brother and his father realized Zeke held much within him. The family patiently waited for him to return to the person he was before striking out for the world of the Englischers.

That night Zeke found it difficult to sleep soundly. He heard his brother's bed creak in the next room. He knew Eli had been sitting in the straight-back chair praying as they had done as children. The bed still had the creaking sound when Eli got into it. The soft snore followed from behind the thin wall. Zeke wished he lived in peace as his brother did. Several times since arriving home, he attempted to pray before bedtime. No words came to him and when he tried to talk with his Gott, he was not sincere. He decided prayer was useless to him. There was no comfort for him. He must work things out in his own way.

If only Sara joined him in his hopes, he thought. Why could he not have the woman he wanted in his life, the opportunity to write about things he learned of and have the security of the Amish way of life, all at the same time?

The day of the barn raising arrived. Droves of buggies arrived at the Breneman farm. The day was crisp but the sun was out. The women and girls unloaded food and went into the house. Some of the young boys helped clear the home to make room for tables and chairs. Then they joined the men at the barn. Sara stood at the kitchen window and looked toward the workers. Zeke pitched in as the others did. Right now he looks just like everyone else out there, she thought.

"We are ready to set the tables," said Katie. "Are you daydreaming?"

Sara looked at her older sister and laughed. "No, I am here to work," she said.

Katie was married and lived a short distance from the family. She was someone Sara often counted on as a good friend as well as her sister who was three years older. Together they worked at setting up the tables.

"I will catch some of the boys," said Ruby Breneman. "They can set a few tables up outside. The men will want to eat and get on with their job."

Ruby healed well and was now using a cane. Her face no longer showed sadness as it had just after Zeke left their home. Sara felt certain his return assisted in his mother's good health.

Sara and Katie went outside to set plates and silverware on the three long tables. The air was much warmer than earlier.

"Gott is gut today," said Sara. "He has sent us warmth and plenty of hot food to feed everyone."

Katie agreed with her. They traded their woolen coats for shawls. The men rolled up their sleeves and continued working until called to eat. The entire framing of the barn was completed.

"We will make gut progress today," said Jonathan. "We are grateful for our neighbors who have come to help. We thank our Gott for them and for sending us this splendid weather."

The men around him agreed and headed for the tables laden with steaming vegetables, fried chicken, roast beef and loaded bowls of boiled potatoes and green beans. Large pitchers of iced tea and lemonade were set along the middle of the tables. Coffee was offered as the men began eating. Then the women fed their children and finally they sat down to enjoy the fruits of their labors.

Sara sat between Katie and her best friend Esther. When the bowls of food started to empty, they took turns replenishing them. Once everyone was fed there was dessert to come. The women brought large cakes and lemon pies to the tables. Applesauce and doughnuts completed the dessert menu.

The rest of the afternoon was spent with the men hammering away and the women cleaning up from the meal. By early evening the barn was completed. Eli and Zeke, with the help of friends, moved the animals from their makeshift shelter into the new barn. They pitched hay into the stalls and filled the water troughs. Before everyone left more food was brought out and everyone consumed the leftovers which made up another meal.

When the Millers arrived home, they took care of needed chores and then all retired earlier than usual. There was no sleeping in the next morning, or any morning. A new day held routine obligations to fulfill.

The next day in late afternoon, Sara filled a bucket of grain ready for Perry and Jacob to feed the chickens when they got home from school. She spoke with her Daed for a few minutes and asked if he needed her help.

"Are you and your Maemm finished inside?" he asked.

"For now we are. Maemm is sewing and I will help her before time for supper preparation."

Eli smiled at his daughter. Together they replenished the troughs and then Sara started back to the house. She heard a buggy coming up the lane. It was too early for Esther to be giving her brothers a ride home. And she rarely did that in winter. She had enough waiting for her at the Clodfelter home before darkness fell.

Her heart leaped when she saw that it was Zeke. He stepped quickly from the buggy and told her he must speak with her. Emma glanced out the window to see the two talking. She decided against intervening with a customary cup of kaffe. Instead, she allowed the time between them. She noticed something amiss between them. Whispering a prayer, she returned to the mending.

"Let us sit over here unless you are cold," said Zeke. He gestured to the bench a few yards away.

"I am fine. The wind is not blowing as fierce," said Sara.

When they settled on the wooden bench, Zeke leaned forward and rested his arms on his knees. He attempted to find words to start his conversation. He finally managed the words.

"Sara, I want to marry you very much. But I do not want to be baptized yet. I am still very confused whether or not I want to join the church."

Sara pulled back in shock. If he wanted to marry her, she thought, he knows he must be baptized and join the church. Her heart beat fast and she felt faint. Regaining composure, she decided compassion was the best approach.

"Perhaps your hesitation is due to your recent return from your experiences in the world," she said. "Give yourself time and you will make the right decision."

"There is something I did not finish telling you. I will tell you what made me come back only to answer one of your first questions." Zeke searched her face to find out if she was willing to listen to more about the world of the Englischers.

"I feel that between us I should understand everything. I am ready to hear anything that explains your actions only if it will benefit our relationship."

"I told you about the man I worked for and how much I wanted to get away from him. I had no idea what kind of job waited for me, but I knew I could no longer remain in that negative environment." Zeke brushed his hand across his forehead. "When I returned to the apartment I found a note from Jason on the table. He had moved out completely. We rented by the month and so it was two weeks until the end of the month. He left me an envelope with plenty of money to continue living there if I wanted to. The note read that if I decided to move on I was to keep the money to find my own way."

Sara surmised the amount of money Jason left for Zeke was quite a bit. She wanted to ask what he did with it all but patiently waited for him to continue.

"It was then I decided my next step. Jason left me enough to go wherever I wanted to go. The next day I told my boss I would not be coming back to work. He was not happy about that and told me so in harsh words. I told the landlord I would not be renting the next month. He was nicer about the news. I do not believe it was hard for him to find renters."

"Where did you go after that?" asked Sara.

"I went to the bus station and bought a ticket for Nebraska. Someone spoke of job opportunities there in the farming industry. I hated farming while I lived here but it was something I knew how to do." Zeke ignored her look of surprise, and again shock, when he told her how much he hated farming. "I landed in North Platte and found a job at a grain elevator. Things were going fine and I was beginning to form words to write. One evening two of the workers invited me to have dinner with them in a restaurant that served steaks. I went with them. They were men I trusted and believed they liked me as well. That night when we left they robbed me of all my money. That included the pay we received earlier that day."

Zeke did not tell Sara he was beaten by the men before they robbed him. They left him for dead in the alley behind the restaurant.

Sara could not believe what she was hearing. Zeke had to learn how cruel the world was by living in it, she thought. She asked him what he did after that. He told her he had mustered enough strength to stumble back to his house. He lived in a small house behind a family's home. The man's parents lived there before they passed away. The next day he started out for work and fell. It was then he mentioned to Sara his bruises from scuffling with the robbers. He did not give full details.

"The farmer's wife saw me and then got me to a doctor. In the waiting room, I decided it was not safe for me to live in the outside world. That is when I decided to find my way home. The man and woman gave me money for the bus. I walked on home from the bus stop and arrived home the night you saw me."

There was much for Sara to take in. No more words of the matter were spoken between them. Sara prayed harder than she ever had that night before she fell asleep.

CHAPTER SEVEN

Speaking Truth

"THESE ARE THE things that ye shall do; Speak ye every man the truth to his neighbour; execute the judgment of truth and peace in your gates: "
Zechariah 8:16

James Bernhard's hands crafted the leg that would fit onto a table. His younger twin sisters swept the shavings from the floor until their mother called them in to help with chores at home. His thoughts went to Sara Miller. He knew he should not be praying she would fall in love with him and choose him for her marriage partner. Instead, he must pray for the will of his Gott. It had been several days since their conversation. By now she must have spoken with Zeke and ironed things out with him. James noted the haggard look in Zeke's eyes even though outwardly he appeared to be fitting back into the Amish community.

Concentrating on his work he ran his hand over the smooth surface. He began carving an indented curve just above the bottom of the table leg. This was the Bernhard signature on every piece of furniture they made. He or his father put this final touch on each piece. The two young men hired to help in their business knew to leave that part to a Bernhard.

He felt, rather than heard, someone come through the door. He glanced up to see Sara Miller as she hesitated in the doorway. Sunrays rested on her slender body. He smiled when he noted a few strands of her blonde hair escaped her cap. They greeted one another with smiles and she joined him.

"I was nearby. I needed some thread at the general store. I hope you do not mind my coming in."

"I do not mind at all," said James. He stood and brushed sawdust off a finished chair and told her to sit down.

"Your work is wunderbarr," she said. "Are you as busy as I last talked with you?"

They had discussed the increased work at the Bernhard shop. James mentioned they were shipping furniture outside the community.

"We are busy." He set the table leg aside.

"I was at the store, but I also wanted to ask if we could see one another this evening," said Sara. "Or if that is not convenient, we will have services at the Kauffmans this Sunday. After the sing and our supper with the other young people, maybe you will drive me home?"

Sara and James knew it was not the custom for the young woman to ask such a favor but in this case, both knew the meaning behind Sara's boldness. James agreed to the Sunday plan. He did not ask if Zeke expected to take her home. Then he recalled not seeing Zeke at church services since he arrived home. His hopes soared at the thought Sara wanted to continue growing their relationship after all.

"I promised you I would talk with you again after speaking with Zeke," she said. "I want to tell you about that."

On the way home Sara felt better that things could be open between her and James. She decided to tell him her decision. She had no plans to discuss the words spoken between her and Zeke. Regret filled her heart when she thought of the expectancy visible in James' eyes. She could not make him wait any longer.

Sunday when everyone gathered at the Kauffmans for services, Sara felt saddened that Zeke chose not to attend. James glanced back at her from across the narrow aisle of chairs set up.

She looked quickly at him and then turned to Esther who sat next to her.

"It is too bad Zeke does not return to services," said Esther in a whisper. "I hope and pray he will soon."

"I do too, Esther. He needs this in his life. He avoids the sings as well."

Services began with a long hymn sung by everyone. There were two longer sermons interspersed with more hymns. When church was over tables and chairs were arranged and food was served. The socialization brought the community together and many visited only on church Sundays. The children chattered together about the upcoming Christmas program they prepared for. Esther told Sara it was hard to keep them focused on their studies they were so excited.

The adults eventually gathered up the young children, along with empty platters and bowls. They left mid afternoon and the young adults talked with each other and sang songs. They then went to the large barn and sat on hay bales and sang more songs. A light supper was spread out for them. After eating they socialized until nine o'clock when James asked Sara if she was ready to go.

Sara ignored Esther's raised eyebrows. She climbed into the wagon and James wrapped blankets around her. Then he gave the horses the signal to move forward. When the goodnight calls from their friends became distant, Sara turned to James.

"I am glad we can have this time together, James. I hope that what I wish to tell you will not be too disappointing."

His spirits sank. She has chosen Zeke after all, he thought. "Whatever your decision is, Sara, I must accept it." He wondered why she decided on Zeke when he was not even baptized. Since he did not attend services, it told him he had no intentions of joining the church.

"When we get to my house, we will go to the barn and talk," she said. "There are extra blankets there for warmth."

When they settled on the hay bales, wrapped in blankets for warmth, Sara spoke.

"James, I do not feel I should marry you since I am not in love with you. You deserve someone who can return the love you have. It has taken a lot of thought and prayer to reach this decision. I am very sorry since I know your wish is to have me for your wife."

James sat still. Then he looked at the woman he loved with all his heart. "Sara, I must accept your decision. My concern is that Zeke may never come into the church. If he is not baptized and does not enter the church you will not be allowed to marry."

Sara twitched a straw between her thumb and index finger. She breathed deeply.

"I do not plan to marry Zeke either," she said. "You are right when you say he may never come into the church. I cannot marry you because, though I value the friendship between us, I do not feel love for you. I cannot marry Zeke because he is not committed to baptism."

She did not express her certainty that Zeke was not committed to the Amish way of life either. When there was no more to say, James reached for Sara's hand to assist her to the floor of the barn. He told her he appreciated her honesty with him. Sadly, it only endeared her more to him.

CHAPTER EIGHT

Peace and Good Will

"AND LET THE peace of God rule in your hearts, to the which also ye are called in one body; and be ye thankful"
Colossians 3:15

Sara fought back tears as she approached the house in darkness. The sounds of James' horse and buggy echoed in her ears. It was no time for doubts. She prayed for the right decision and knew prayers were answered.

In the following week, she thought less of Zeke. Their paths did not cross since there was no reason they should. Convinced that Zeke was not the man she once believed him to be assuaged some of her loss. The days grew colder and Christmas neared. Members of her community exchanged small gifts within their own families. The celebration included a large meal and lots of cookies. Sara and her mother baked them by the dozens. They mixed candies and placed them on trays to harden.

Jacob was excited about his part in the Christmas program at school. "Everyone is invited," he told his family night after night. They assured him they would not miss it. The ten year old ran into the kitchen after helping with chores.

"Slow down, Jacob," said his Maemm. "Do not run so." He reached for a candy. "And do not eat candy. It is not ready yet. Let it get hard first."

Emma wondered about the energy her youngest child had. She vowed to speak to Eli that night about giving their son more responsibilities. Perhaps that would help to expend some of his vigor. That evening when the family gathered in the sitting room for prayer, Jacob asked his parents if he could recite his poem to them before prayers. It was hard to tell him no.

"After all," said Eli, "Christmas comes only once a year. This time next year Jacob will not be so eager to recite in front of us."

They all laughed but Jacob could not imagine getting too old for something like that. The poem was short and he had it memorized perfectly. He smiled broadly when he finished.

"I guess since everyone has heard your poem, they will not be going to our program," said Perry.

Jacob's face dropped.

"Perry, do not tease your bruder," said Emma. "Of course we will be there. Now it is time for our nightly prayers."

Eli picked up his Bible and began leading his family in prayer. Later when Sara submerged herself under the quilts she thought of the small embroidered doily she finished for her mother. For Perry and Jacob she bought writing paper and a new pencil for each of them. She was sure her father would be pleased with the white cotton handkerchief, hemmed with perfect stitches. He could tuck it into the pocket of his Sunday trousers for use if needed. Her eyelids fluttered and she sank into a deep sleep.

The day finally arrived for the Christmas program at the schoolhouse. When the Millers arrived there were several buggies already there. While the children prepared for their entrance the families chatted with one another. Sara glanced around and saw that Esther's father and Isaac were seated together. Next to them were Esther's brother Silas and his wife Marian. Ruth Clodfelter was not there. It was no surprise to Sara since she knew Ruth's health deteriorated more each day. The Brenemans came for the event even though they no longer had children in school. Zeke was absent.

Esther stood in front of the group and got everyone's attention. She announced the poems to be recited by which child. Then she told the audience there would be a surprise at the end. Jacob was third to recite his part. He was a natural in front of a crowd. Perry and several older children his age sang songs about giving love at Christmas. There were more recitations of stories and poems until the last child spoke. Esther moved them all to the back of the room under the blackboard. They stood in a line against the wall and she motioned for two boys to go out through the back door. They returned with straw and a small cradle. Other children quickly draped shawls and covers over their shoulders and clustered around the cradle. They all recited a verse from St. Luke that told the story of Christmas. When the program ended, everyone expressed how wonderful it was.

Sara approached Esther. "When did you have time to put all of this together and teach at the same time?"

Esther smiled her thanks and told Sara she was not so sure learning took place the last few weeks. They were distracted at the sounds of chairs scraping on the floor. A table centered the room and was laden with Christmas treats. Candies and cookies were being passed around to everyone. Sara stood with her friend behind the teacher's desk and poured lemonade for those who came up to congratulate her on a job well done.

"It was wunderbarr Esther and amazing you managed to get them all in order."

The voice was familiar to Sara and she smiled at James. His sisters had recited a poem together. Sara took a second glance at James when he locked eyes with Esther. She smiled to herself. In spite of her vow not to marry yet, Esther may have to eat her words, thought Sara. It suddenly dawned on her that Esther and James would make a perfect couple. She must speak to Esther about that possibility.

The following day was Christmas. Katie and her family arrived for the large dinner that Emma and Sara prepared. Katie brought in more cookies and a steaming roast with potatoes and carrots. They ate together and it was the one time in the year there were no chores other than caring for animals.

They congregated in the sitting room after the meal. Some of the food was left on the dining room table for guests who would drift in for visits. Emma lit three red candles. The family caught up on each others' lives. Several buggies came up the lane toward the house. The Clodfelters and Kauffmans arrived at the same time. Emma went to the kitchen and put on more coffee. While everyone talked at the same time, Esther helped Sara pour lemonade.

"Pass the cookies around, too, Esther," said Emma.

The comfort of neighbors and family together on this day made Sara think how wonderful her life was. Even though everyone said 'no thank you, I cannot eat another bite' they did anyway. The Millers planned to visit neighbors the next day. The community celebrated Christmas for two days. The young adults looked forward to celebration of the holiday into January. Socials and visiting continued in between necessary work tasks.

Esther drew her friend aside. "Sara, I hope you do not mind, but James has asked to court me."

Sara hugged her friend. "Of course I do not mind. But I must ask you what happened to your vow to not marry."

They laughed and then Esther grew serious. "My Daed spoke with me a few weeks ago. He told me to find someone to marry and that I should not feel obligated to allow my family to come first in this case." Esther wrung her hands and then relaxed. "He meant for me to think about myself before it was too late. As you know Maemm is not well. She eats less each day and often sinks in and out of consciousness. We do not feel she will last much longer in this world."

Sara took her friend's hand and pulled her upstairs to her room. They sat on the bed and Esther continued.

"I worry about Letty. She will soon be eight years old. She is too young to take over household duties. Isaac is a hard worker and helps our Daed in every way. James is interested in courting me seriously. I do not know which way to turn."

Sara suggested they pray before they talk it over further. They bowed their heads and asked Gott to lead Esther in the right way. When they finished Esther looked at Sara and smiled.

"Praying is always the way. He will lead the way," she said.

Sara agreed with her. "If James and you are meant for each other then Gott will find a way to care for Letty and your family. I am so sorry about your Maemm. I know she suffers much."

"Silas and Marian come often and help with things. But Marian's boppli is due to arrive in two months. Besides, she has enough to keep her own household running."

"I will do whatever you need," said Sara.

Esther thanked her and told her James had not spoken of marriage and so maybe she was ahead of the matter. They had been courting for two weeks before Christmas and they liked each other. Esther felt a love growing for him. For the first time she desired a husband and family of her own. She hoped James was her answer.

"It helps that James lives at the next farm from ours," said Esther. "It is close for him to come over. I want to tell Maemm about him but she does not seem to know what is going on around her."

Sara felt sorry for Esther. She and her mother had never had a close relationship. Sara could not imagine not having her own mother to confide in. Esther sometimes spoke briefly of serious matters with Emma but did not wish to burden her with her problems. Emma understood the loss Esther experienced in not having a mother to talk things over with.

When Christmas night fell over the Miller house everyone expressed gratitude for the blessed day they enjoyed with family and neighbors.

Sara wondered if Zeke enjoyed Christmas in the same manner with his family as she did with hers.

CHAPTER NINE

The Mission of the Heart

*"THE LORD IS my portion, saith my soul;
therefore will I hope in him."*
Lamentations 3:24

Zeke Breneman lay back on his feather bed and searched for peace within himself. There was none. This Christmas he endured the activity of the holidays. His family was immersed in the day; he only pretended. He did not want to disturb his mother's happiness with the Christmas celebrations and so he made the effort to be joyful with them. Neighbors visited throughout the afternoon. His mother spent the last week baking bread puddings, cookies and loaves of bread. She made their traditional candies in preparation for family and visitors alike. He gathered with his parents and Eli each evening in prayer. His lips moved but not his heart. This Christmas was no different than any other day for him.

The next day brought more celebrations. The Brenemans planned to visit others in the community as was their tradition. That morning after breakfast Ruby asked her husband to spare Zeke for a few minutes. Zeke questioned his mother with unspoken words.

"Zeke, I wish to speak with you privately," said his mother when Eli and Jonathan left for the barn. "You have come home but you are not happy. Do you miss the outside world?"

Zeke shook his head vehemently. "I do not miss the world, Maemm. I want to fit in again but something prevents me. I am old enough to be baptized and join the church but I do not wish to do that. I am sorry I have disappointed you."

Ruby reached for her son's hands and clasped them in hers. "You do not disappoint me. You were brave enough to realize your mistake and you came home where you belong. When you say something is missing, you are right, Zeke. Your missing link is your connection with Gott."

Mother and son sat in silence. Zeke spoke first. "I believe you, Maemm, but I cannot bring myself to pray. I feel Gott led me to his beauty in the nature of the outside world. I aspire to write about it for others to enjoy. I cannot do that in the Amish world.

"Until you return to prayer, Zeke, nothing in your life will have meaning; not this writing you speak of, or belonging with the family and our community."

She stood to clear the table. Zeke left her and joined his father and brother in the barn. They talked the night before of visiting the Millers and Clodfelters today. His father spoke of stopping by the Bernhards as well. Zeke's brother told him James Bernhard no longer courted Sara and instead was seeing Esther. He knew he could refuse to go with his family but he did not want to hurt them by not joining them.

At the Clodfelters they were welcomed by Esther and Letty. Jacob Clodfelter and his son Isaac welcomed them into the sitting room. Letty presented a tray of cookies for everyone. Ruby complimented her on the taste of them. The little girl smiled and told them she helped Esther make every one of them. While they enjoyed the company, Esther noted Zeke's fake interactions with others in celebration. She whispered a silent prayer for him. Everyone in the community prayed for him, she thought. She was relieved he had not been baptized and was easily accepted back by all. Zeke caught her eye and noticed compassion in hers. He did not want people to feel sorry for him. He realized Esther was concerned about him and thought more highly of her when he came to that conclusion. She would make a good wife someday for James Bernhard, he thought.

After an hour of visiting, the Brenemans wished the family a happy Christmas. As they left, more families were coming toward the Clodfelter house. Zeke noticed one buggy held the Miller family. The families called out to one another as they passed. Zeke's heart beat faster when he and Sara locked eyes.

Once she saw Zeke again, Sara knew what had to be done. Whether he accepted what she had in mind or not was another question. She knew she could not fail in her plans to help him. She realized how hopeless Zeke felt. His eyes told her that. But she also knew that the God they served was a God of all hope.

When he refused to go to church or join the sings, she decided at the time he did not want to get better. Now when she met his eyes, she resolved to make him her mission. She knew her love for him remained deep within her heart. She would not give up on him. Zeke was a gut man, she thought. He simply was misdirected. She must get him back on track with their Gott. Instead of ignoring him, it was her wish and her duty to help him find his way back to her and to the Amish way of life. Either Zeke Breneman would decide on baptism and join the church, or he would sink deeper into hopelessness. She could not let the latter happen.

Nothing is impossible, Sara told herself, and faith rose in her heart that the prodigal would not only return in body, but in heart and soul.

She was sure of it.

***

THE END

Thank you so much for reading, and following the unfolding story of Zeke and Sara. For a wonderfully happy ending, and to see how God works all things together for good, even Zeke's restless wandering heart, read the third and final book in the Homeward Bound Series, 'Love Is My Home'. It is available on Amazon for just $0.99 or free with Kindle Unlimited.

You can also enjoy the first chapter right now. I have included it as a BONUS at the end of this book. Enjoy!

CHAPTER TEN

Bonus Chapter – Homeward Bound Book 3

Chapter 1 – Love is my Home

Sara Miller awoke to sun that broke through the gauze curtains on her bedroom window. With renewed vigor, she rushed to the window and noted small purple crocuses emerging from the ground. Light snow gave the background to the first tiny signs of Spring.

"Our Gott will replenish all of us," she said aloud.

Emma smiled at her daughter's animated face when she entered the kitchen. Like Sara, she looked forward to warmer seasons. Today they would plan the garden. It was too early to plant but she and Sara could make plans for it.

"I would like to plant a few herbs this year, Maemm," said Sara. "Perhaps some lavender, and mint is gut, too. Mint is delicious in tea, especially iced tea in the summertime."

"We will think of vegetables first. Last season gave plenty to keep us fed over the winter months. We can use some herbs as well."

Sara agreed. She began helping her mother prepare breakfast for her two brothers and her father. The boys would soon be out of school for the summer. Eli needed them to help plant the corn and alfalfa. When they came in from the barn, it seemed everyone was glad for the new season.

Monday was laundry day and once the tubs were filled with hot water Sara began washing while her mother cleaned up the house. Together they would rinse the clothes and hang them on the lines to dry. As Sara went through the rhythmic motions of scrubbing the family's clothing, she thought of Zeke Brenneman. She had prayed hard all winter long for his return to Gott.

"I am here to help you finish, Dochtah," said Emma, interrupting her thoughts.

She knew Sara thought about Zeke and prayed he would find restoration. After he returned from the outside world he was restless. Sara told her he was not ready for Baptism. That meant they could not marry until he gave himself to Gott and joined the Amish church. Emma rarely interfered in her daughter's life unless Sara asked her for advice. This morning she broke that resolve and felt she must point something out to Sara.

"Sara, continue praying for Zeke but you must realize that in the end he will have to find his own way back. You cannot do that for him."

"I know that, Maemm," said Sara. "I am sure that Gott will take full control of Zeke. I love him very much and I know he feels the same about me. I will wait and see what happens."

They continued hanging clothes, each in their own thoughts. The gentle wind caused the clothes to billow in the soft air. Snow previously on the ground gave way to small brown spots in the earth. A hint of green attempted to burst through the dormant grass. Sara tilted her head to the cobalt blue sky and peace rushed through her.

That same morning Zeke Brenneman awoke with a strange feeling. Baffled as to what the sentiment meant, he accepted the calm that washed over him. His mind had been in an uproar throughout the previous months. He was glad to be home again but he had not found his way back to the Gott his family followed and believed in. Looking out his window, he saw the same incredible vista Sara witnessed from her own bedroom. Spring suddenly emerged from the long winter. That must be it, he thought. It is spring that causes this feeling within me. He dressed and went to join his brother and father. His younger brother Eli walked with anticipation noted by his brisk stride.

Zeke marveled at Eli. He courted Anna Kauffman and focused on a life ahead with her. Eli loved farm life. He melded with the soil and crops in a way that suggested both the earth and Eli were one and the same. A real Adam, a man of the ground; a man of Eden. Zeke did chores and tasks expected but his heart had never been into farming. Always a dreamer of sorts, he was pulled toward being more an observer of nature rather than a participant. After milking the cows and feeding the animals, the three men returned to the house for a hearty breakfast.

"Your Maemm is the best cook in the country," said Jonathan of his wife. He knew he should not be lauding her virtues but it was his way of teaching his sons how to respect the women they would one day marry. He often told them to practice humility. The compliment he gave his wife should not interfere with that virtue, he reasoned.

"You say that every morning when we are starving," said Eli. He laughed at his humor and Zeke joined in.

"Jah, I do that, but she knows how to prepare gut food for us," said their father.

The aroma of sizzling bacon and hot muffins sped their way to the kitchen. Ruby noted that Zeke was more relaxed today. She breathed a silent prayer of thanksgiving. Gott answered her prayers.

Jonathan told his sons to check all of the fences for any breaks. They were ready to put the increased head of cows in a new pasture. It was the one saved for grasses for the animals to feed on. His sons left for the pasture and reached the end of the property.

"Are you finally getting interested in mending fences, Zeke?" asked his brother.

"Why do you ask that? It is no secret I do not enjoy farmwork."

"I asked you because you look happier than you have for a long time. I just thought you were finally becoming a real farmer."

Eli had a sense of humor, thought Zeke, and he laughed with his brother. Even Zeke knew it was the first time in a long while that a genuine laugh escaped his lips. He had no idea what was happening to him. Eli smiled to himself. The family prayed hard for Gott to bring his bruder back to them. Apparently, renewal for Zeke was in progress. His thoughts shifted to Anna Kauffman. Eli and Anna talked of marriage. They would be baptized at the same time. When summer arrived, they would start lessons together. His prayer today was that Zeke would join them.

That evening after supper, the Brenemans sat together in the sitting room. Jonathan retrieved his Bible and began the nightly prayers. Zeke bowed his head and listened to his father's steady voice. Tonight he paid attention to the words spoken. "Ask and it will be given to you; seek and you will find; knock and the door will be opened to you. For everyone who asks receives; the one who seeks finds; and to the one who knocks, the door will be opened."

Jonathan closed the Bible. The family went to their rooms after listening to Jonathan discuss the verse, followed by prayer. The words from the Bible stuck in Zeke's mind as he drifted off to sleep.

Sara and her family also prayed before bedtime as was the custom. Her father opened the family Bible. Eli chose a verse from Psalms: "He guides the humble in what is right and teaches them his way."

When Sara rested her head on her pillow the words continued to flow through her mind. I must be humble in my thoughts for Zeke's peace, she thought. It is not up to me to carry out a plan; I must remember to leave that to Gott. Everything is his plan and he will teach us all his way. That includes Zeke.

Pick-up a copy of Homeward Bound by Grace Given to continue reading.

ABOUT THE AUTHOR

Grace Given is an author of sweet, Christian Amish Romance.

For as long as I can remember I have been fascinated by the simplicity and faith of the Amish people. In a world so busy and self-consumed, the virtues of a simple life are more and more appealing to many people.

Amish romance has given me the opportunity to express my own heart's desire for a world less cluttered, where love and virtue abound.

Thank you for choosing a PureRead Romance. As a way to thank you we would also like to give you a special novella, Grace Abounding.

http://pureread.com/gracegiven

OTHER BOOKS BY GRACE GIVEN

SWEET ROMANCE
Homeward Bound
Timeless Amish Love Stories
Angel's Among Us
Abrams Child
Angels Among Us Series

ROMANTIC MYSTERY
Amish Assault On The Highway
Stranger In The Woods

Thank you so much for reading.

READ ALL OF GRACE'S BOOKS

pureread.com/gracegivenbooks

CPSIA information can be obtained
at www.ICGtesting.com
Printed in the USA
BVHW062235180820
586749BV00011BA/331